STICKS AND STONES

ANN MALASPINA

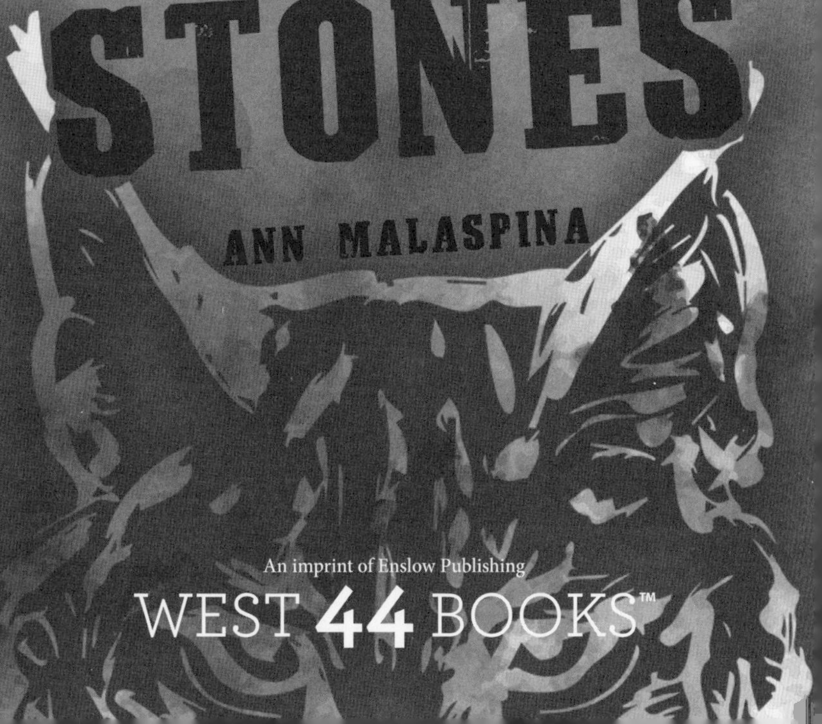

An imprint of Enslow Publishing
WEST 44 BOOKS™

Please visit our website, www.west44books.com.
For a free color catalog of all our high-quality books, call toll free 1-800-398-2504.

Cataloging-in-Publication Data
Names: Malaspina, Ann.
Title: Sticks and stones / Ann Malaspina.
Description: Buffalo, NY : West 44, 2027. | Series: West 44 MG verse
Identifiers: ISBN 9781978598713 (pbk.) | ISBN 9781978598706 (library bound) | ISBN 9781978598720 (ebook)
Subjects: LCSH: School--Fiction. | Social groups--Fiction. | Interpersonal relations--Fiction.
Classification: LCC PZ7.1.M353 St 2027 | DDC [F]--dc23

First Edition

Published in 2027 by
Enslow Publishing
2544 Clinton Street
Buffalo, NY 14224

Editor: Caitie McAneney
Designer: Tanya Dellaccio Keeney

Photo Credits: Cover (bobcat) vir ivlev/Shutterstock.com.

Printed in the United States of America

CPSIA compliance information: Batch #CS27W44: For further information contact Enslow Publishing LLC at 1-800-398-2504.

For Rob, Sam, and Nick

BOBCAT

The bobcat stops
between a scarlet oak
and a pitch pine.

Lifting a paw, she sniffs . . .
the tang of pine sap,
the stink of a skunk,
and the sweet smell of a boy
who had pancakes for breakfast.

A pine warbler trills in the September air.

A black rat snake
slides into the pond.

The boy’s sneakers
crunch on dry pine needles.

And the bobcat runs.

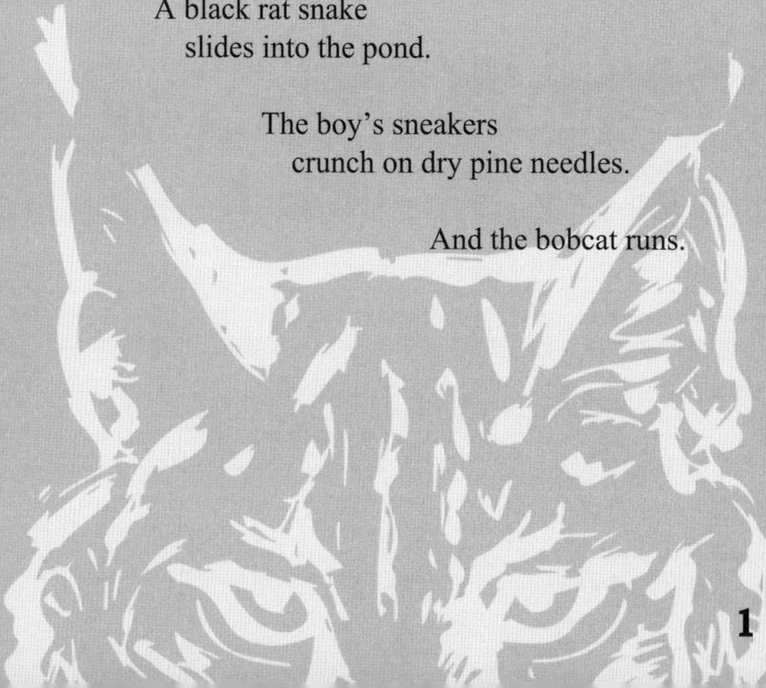

CHARLIE

What was that animal?

A stray cat?
Haunches too strong.

A raccoon?
Legs too long.

A BOBCAT?

Dad says bobcats are rare.
Highly endangered.

"You can live your whole life
in the New Jersey Pine Barrens
and never see a single one," he says.

If that was a bobcat, maybe it will bring me luck.

FIRST DAY

I take off through the woods.

Up the hill and across the back field

of Pinelands Middle School.

It's the first day of sixth grade.

And if sixth grade is anything like fifth grade,

I will need all the luck in the universe.

NAMES

Mr. Friedlander calls out names.
But no one's listening.

Thirty-one kids in homeroom
and everyone's talking at once.

I slip into a desk in the back
next to the window.

A girl wearing a Mets cap
comes in after me.

With no desks left, Mr. F points to
a stool by the sink.

Over the noise, he calls out
every name twice.

"Charlie Hooser?
CHARLIE HOOSER?"

Someone snickers.
"Hooser the Loser!"

Same as every year.
I raise my hand. "Here."

BRIANNA

"Ouch!"

It's Brianna, our class queen,
pinching my arm in the crowded hall.

I freeze.

Her eyes are glaciers. Blue and icy.

"After school.
Victor's Candies.
Only losers are late."

I just learned something new.
Glaciers don't blink.

DAMAGE

I check my arm for damage.

Four red
fingermarks
and a thumbprint.

Before I look up again,
Glacier Eyes is gone.

WHY?

It's not my first Brianna pinch.

The first was last year.

They (Brianna and her bestie Maya)
were chasing us (me and Kev) after gym class.

Was it because Kev's the only kid in gym
who does a better handspring than Brianna?

Or because I'm too chicken to even try one?

I should know by now.
There doesn't have to be a WHY.

Today is different.
She wants to meet me someplace.

So, WHY?

KEV

Kev waits for me at our usual table.
In the back of the cafeteria,
next to the fake palm tree.

"It's the Team. It must be," he says, chewing
on a chicken nugget. "I'm soooo jealous!"

The Team.

A sixth-grade tradition.
The secret club no one talks about.

Could it be true?

I never get picked for anything. Neither does Kev.

Hooser's a loser,
Kev's a . . . he's just Kev.

"Soooo jealous," my best friend says again.

THE ROCK

I don't notice
the girl who was late for homeroom
sitting at the end of our table
until lunch is almost over.

She leaves a stone on her chair.
Gray, round, and smooth.
It fits perfectly
in my hand.

SECRETS

Victor’s Candies is squeezed between the pizza place and the antique store on Broad Street.

Today, Kev stops before we get there.
“You gotta tell me everything!”

I look down at my old green sneakers from last year.

Mom said we had to wait on buying a new pair.

I don’t think I can tell Kev anything.
That’s what a secret club’s all about.

SECRETS.

“Sure.” I lie.

BETTER OR NOT

Watching Kev walk away, I feel a rush.
Like when I jump in a pool
in the middle of summer.

Is this what my brother Mikey felt
when he got picked
for the varsity football team?

Like he's better than
everyone who did not
make the team?

I'm not better than Kev.
But I am kind of sick
of being loser me.

LICORICE

The sign says:

First Day of School
Half-Price Candy Sale!

Crowds of kids and bins of candy fill the small store.

Gummy bears.
Caramels.
Red Hots.
Choco-Bits.

I finally find the black licorice.

"Eww! Licorice is disgusting!" Brianna says.

Wrong, Brianna! Licorice is my favorite.

But I dump out my bag anyway . . .

Because Charlie Hooser can change.
Because maybe this year it will be different.
Because, for once, I might be lucky.

. . . and reach for the sour balls.

CARAMEL

Lucas shoves a caramel in my face.

He's the fastest runner in our class.
Fast enough to trip Kev at recess.
So fast, no one sees Lucas do it.
Except for me.

The caramel hurts my teeth.

I hope Lucas isn't on the Team.

THE TEAM

Sixth graders only.
Some sixth graders only.

You must be:

Picked out.
Pulled over.
Pinched.

We're crowded in the alley
behind the candy store.

Maya, Tomas, Alyssa, Derek . . . and Lucas.

"Out of 120 kids, we're the lucky seven," Brianna says.

Her breath smells like peppermint—
and not in a good way.

More like . . .

Peppermint is better than licorice,
and I am better than you.

I suck on a sour lime ball.

RULERS

Brianna tells everyone to be quiet.
"I'm calling the meeting to order."

"Why are you the president?" Lucas blurts out.

Brianna tosses her ponytail. "It's a family tradition."

Her older sister was president last year.

"You're, like, part of a royal family!" Maya says.

"I kind of am." Brianna pumps her fist.

"The Team rules!"

I have a funny feeling in the pit of my stomach.
Like I'm part of something big.
Something important.

Then I remember
how much my mom hates royalty.
She says the United States
doesn't want a queen or king.

But being a Ruler is better than
being a pathetic Loser any day!

"The Team rules!" we shout back.

PLEDGE OF SILENCE

When we raise
our right hands
and promise
not to
tell,

all I can think of is:

Tell what?

MIKEY

"Were you on the Team?"

When your brother's bed is three feet away,
it's hard to keep secrets.

Usually, Mikey pretends I don't exist.
I'm the weirdo brother who can't catch a football.

But I need to know what he knows.

Mikey turns on the light.
"What the heck, Charlie!"

I think that means "yes."

"The Team used to be cool," he says.
"Jokes and pranks and harmless stuff . . ."

The light goes off.
"Quit now, little bro . . . before it's too late."

Too late for what?

GROWL

A low growl wakes me up.

It's not Mikey.
He's a snorer, not a growler.

The sound comes from far away.
Some place deep in the pinelands.

I'm thinking: bobcat.

Bobcats don't join teams,
but they sure sound lonely.

EGG WHITES

"I think I heard a bobcat last night," I say at breakfast.

Dad looks up from his egg whites.

Ever since his heart attack, he can't eat whole eggs.

Or butter.
Or ice cream.
Or anything good.

He dumps the egg whites in the sink.

"I might have seen one too!" I add.

Back on the couch, Dad clicks on the TV.

DAD

Dad wasn't always a couch potato.

When he wasn't at his construction company,
he was out in the woods—
finding rare mushrooms,
spotting migrating birds,
paddling his canoe.

Now, he doesn't go out, except to the doctor's office.

MOM

Since Dad's not working,
Mom has to take double shifts at the hospital.

She's a nurse in the emergency room.

Sometimes I see her looking at Dad
like she doesn't know who he is anymore.

I don't think Dad knows who he is either.

ART

is always my worst class.

I spill the paint.
My clay pots crack.
I have NO artsy ideas.

Looks like the new girl (her name is Mitzy,
from Brooklyn) is the opposite.

Today, she's sketching furiously.
Her charcoal pencil bleeds
onto the paper like blood!

I take the stone out of my pocket. "Is this yours?"

MITZY DOESN'T ANSWER

"Was that you in the woods today?" she asks, instead.

I took my usual path to school.
A baby rattlesnake surprised me from
under a rock.

"Why were you there?" I ask.

Mitzy shrugs. "It's not like you own the pinelands."

I never said I did!

I guess she doesn't want her stupid stone.

BLACKPINK

Kev plops down between us.

Sunglasses sit on top of his head.
His hair's blown out like a K-pop star.

"What's your favorite group?" Mitzy asks him.

"Blackpink," Kev says.

Mitzy hums and Kev sings the words
to a song I kind of know.

I duck my head.
Singing in art class is NOT cool!

WHY

would anyone move here from Brooklyn?

To watch the blueberries turn blue?

To see the truckers drive down Route 9
on their way to someplace else?

Dad says the Pine Barrens are
the most precious 1.1 million acres
in the whole country.

Sandy soil, scrubby pine
and oak forests, clean rivers
and wetlands.

All protected by law.

“It’s a national treasure,” Dad says.

Most people I know have always lived here.

But unless you like mosquitoes and ticks,
I don’t know why you’d want to *move* here.

DRAWINGS

The art teacher, Mrs. Lopez, calls out,
"Five more minutes, and then we share."

Mitzy is drawing a pile of stones.
Kev is drawing a map of South Korea.

They're both humming.

When we hand in our drawings,
Mitzy asks me, "Is that a tail?"

"No."

"Hmm," she says.

Mrs. Lopez says we're going to be drawing
for the next six weeks!

BLUE SUBARU

"Charlie!"

Mom's blue Subaru blocks the bus lane.

"I want you to take Dad
for a walk today."

Brianna and Maya are coming toward the car.

"Are those girls waving at you?"

I forgot about the Team meeting!

"Your dad needs you!" Mom calls.

The Subaru doesn't move, watching me.

WATCH ME

The seven of us are back in the alley.
"I found our first target," Brianna is saying.

First target?

Alyssa bites her thumbnail.

I don't know what's happening.

Derek's face turns red.
"We need to take out the weirdos!"

Now I'm the one biting my nails.

"Weirdness is like a disease," Brianna agrees.
"You can catch it if you get too close."

She's staring at me like I'm contagious!

WEIRDO

No doubt. I'm the weirdo here.

Hooser the Loser.
The kid who can't catch a football
or dribble a soccer ball.

The kid who's too short.
Too skinny.
Too quiet.

"Why am I even on the Team?" I mutter.

"It's about the lock," Maya whispers.
The lock?

Now I remember.

LOCK JAM

It's fifth grade . . .

Brianna has a fit at her locker.
Her lock is jammed.
Even the janitor can't open it.

Me: "I can do it."
Brianna: "Hooser? I doubt it."

I turn the lock slowly.
Listen for the silent clicks.
My hands feel powerful, like they're magic.

The lock slips open
and everyone cheers.

For exactly one minute, I'm not weird at all.

Is that all there is?

Nothing special about Charlie Hooser—
except he can open locks?

Is that why I was chosen?

THE DOCTOR SAYS

heart attacks can hurt more than your heart.
They can make you feel sad, or even afraid.

        Maybe that's the reason
Dad's stuck on the couch,
                watching shows about popping pimples.

"He needs to get up," Mom says again today.

        So he can get strong.
So he can go back to work.
                So he isn't afraid anymore.

"Charlie, take your father outdoors!"

BARBECUE CHIPS

Dad's watching a stupid show about hoarders.

A bag of barbecue chips sits on his lap.

"Do you want to go for a walk?" I ask.

But he clicks the TV even louder.

I slam the door and grab my mountain bike.

RIDING IN THE PINES

The roads through the Pine Barrens
are made for dirt bikes. Flat, sandy,
and wide enough for two riders.

But it’s easy to get lost in there.
Acres of oak and piney woods all look the same.
Some people don’t come back.

Kev and I never get lost.
We’ve been riding the sandy roads
since we were little.

He’s faster, always out front.
I like to stop to look at things.
But we always stay close.

Today is different.
Kev lags behind like he’s mad.
When he catches up, he does a wheelie.

Sand spatters in my face.

TELL ME

"Are you gonna tell me?" Kev asks.
"Tell you what?"
"The Team, Charlie. Tell me about the Team."

I don't know what to tell him.
About contagious weirdos?
And how I don't want to be one anymore?

Crows circle over a swampy bog.
"Caw! Caw! Caw!"
They're mad at me too.

BLACKBERRIES

We ride past the pond with the snapping turtles.

In a prickly thicket,
we grab the last blackberries
the birds left behind.

Kev rolls his bike over a log.

He rides faster and faster.
I can barely keep up.
Then he brakes suddenly.

I crash into him.

"Watch out!"

"Watch out yourself!"

STONE PILE

In the open clearing,

who do we see?

It's Mitzy, wearing a Mets cap.

What the heck?

She's lifting bricks and stones into a pile. "Hey, guys."

"Why are you here?" I ask.

"I live here."

Hidden in the pines is a beat-up house trailer.

"Sweet," Kev says.

TRAILER

I stare at the trailer.

Vines cover the backside.
Pine trees crowd it, casting shadows.

The windows are painted black.
A rainbow flag flies from the roof.

"Have you heard growling at night?" I ask.

GROWLING

Mitzy stops smiling. "What do you mean?"

"The bobcat," I say. "Have you heard her?"

Kev is curious. "What did you THINK
Charlie meant?"

"Mr. Dangerous," she says.
"Why do you THINK
I'm collecting stones?"

Two more are in her hands.

TURNS OUT

there are good reasons to move
from Brooklyn
to the Pine Barrens.

"Mr. Dangerous"
is Mitzy's mom's
ex-boyfriend.

He never hit Mitzy.
But he hit
her mom.

Mitzy says that
he won't leave them alone.
"He's a stalker."

After we help her
pile up
more stones,

we cover them
with sticks
and pine needles.

Sticks and stones.

TOP STONE

The top stone teeters for a second
and then sits still.

It's a stockpile of weapons,
for Mitzy to defend her home.

If the pile falls over,
someone could get hurt.

Badly.

"Yes, they could," Mitzy says.
"Do you want to meet my mom?"

SAFE HAVEN

In a patch of dirt, her mom is planting marigolds.
"Hey," she says, when Mitzy introduces us.

The trailer is just yards from Route 9.
The speeding traffic comes way too close.

"This was Mitzy's great uncle's property," she explains.
"We're hoping to build a house here."

She says the Pine Barrens were a safe haven
for enslaved people seeking freedom.

"Some of them were our ancestors," Mitzy says.
Then she passes around a bag of cheese balls.

JERSEY DEVIL

Riding home, Kev shouts out,
"It's like the Jersey Devil!"

My front wheel trips over a stump
and I almost fall over.

The Jersey Devil is an old folktale
about a monster who lurks in the Pine Barrens.

Its creepy claws, wings, and strange
misshapen body couldn't be worse than Mr. Dangerous.

I hope neither one shows up anytime soon.

ON TUESDAY

Mr. F leaves the classroom to use the restroom.

We're supposed to read quietly.
"Eyes on the page!" he tells us.

Leaning over, Lucas whispers, "It's Moses."

Moses? I hardly know him.
But he's never called me a loser.
Or pinched me.

When I ask why, Lucas shrugs.

"Take a guess."

MICKEY MOUSE

It has to be his cap.

The Mickey Mouse cap
with black plastic

Mickey Mouse ears.

It's not a cap for a sixth grader.
More like for a six-year-old.

No one knows why Moses wears it everyday
until Brianna rips it off.

Now, we all know.

EMERGENCY!

Moses's scream is a fire engine siren
ripping through Mr. F's homeroom.

Emergency!

Blasting like a mega-alarm.
Breaking our ear drums.

Emergency!

We cover our ears . . .

Emergency!

. . . but we can't cover our eyes.

ZOMBIES

Moses has no hair.

Not even around the edges like Dad and Mr. F.

No one says anything.
No one does anything.
No one moves an inch.

We're all zombies, except Mitzy.

She jumps off her stool by the window.
"Come with me," she says,
grabbing Moses's hand.

METS CAP

When they get back, Moses wears
Mitzy's blue and orange Mets cap.

He looks at the floor,
but Mitzy looks straight at Brianna.

Mitzy's eyes are on fire.

OWN IT

Turns out, Moses had cancer when he was younger.
He's okay now, but his hair never grew back.

Brianna isn't sorry. Not one bit.

"If I didn't have hair, I would own it."
Miss Glacier Eyes twists her
thick ponytail.

Alyssa tugs her braid, looking away.
But Maya nods, like her bestie is a wise queen.

Yeah, right.

NEVER

Mickey Mouse never hurt anybody.

That’s what Mitzy says too.
“How could you, Charlie?”

Hey! How does she know I’m on the Team?

Kev interrupts us.
“Sorry, Charlie. I had to tell her.”

DIDN'T KNOW

The only reason Mitzy doesn't
totally hate me . . .

is because I didn't know
what Brianna was going to do.

It's true. I didn't.
But when I try to explain . . .

her eyes roll.
"If that makes you feel better."

200 WORDS

Mr. F makes us stay in from recess
and take out our language arts notebooks.
"I want you to write a two-hundred-word essay:
Why Kindness Matters."

Even Moses has to do it,
which makes no sense to me.
Then again, he didn't HAVE TO
always wear that stupid cap.

THE WORLD IS A MESS

It takes me a long time to write anything.

Then I remember when Mom told Dad
for the millionth time to get off the couch.

“The world is a mess,” Dad grumbled. “Why should I?”

I’ve got my title. *The World Is a Mess.*

Then I start writing: *That’s why it’s better to be kind.*

NOT ME

Me: What did the Team do when you were on it?

Mikey: Well . . . we egged the principal's house.

Me: Why did you do that?

Mikey: He took away the school soda machines.

Me: You don't even drink soda!

Mikey: . . .

Me: Did ***you*** throw eggs?

Mikey: Not me, exactly.

I know what he means. It wasn't him. It was the Team.

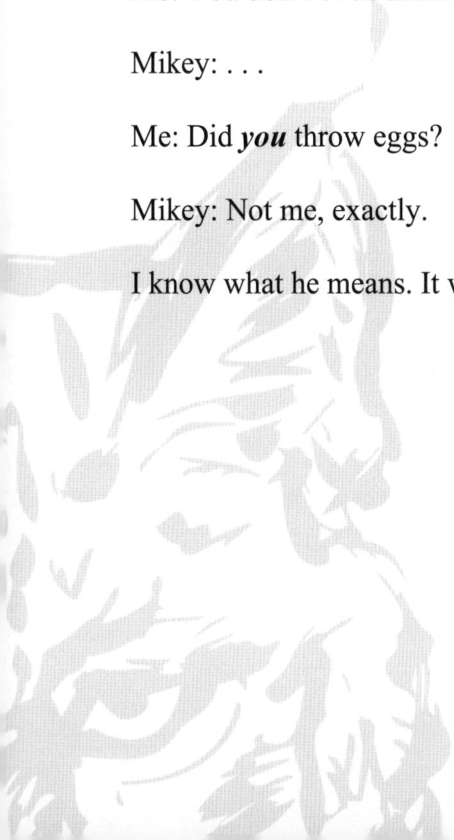

WEDNESDAY

Mitzy and Kev eat lunch outside.
I eat alone with the fake palm tree.

Then Brianna sits down.

So do Lucas, Maya,
and the rest of the Team.

I have that funny feeling again.
Like I'm part of something bigger.

Something important.

Derek unpeels a banana.
"So, who's next?"

BOBCAT

The boy is near.

She hears his heartbeat.
She senses his curiosity.

The bobcat has known people before.

One pointed a gun at her.
Another chased her into the river.

But she's kept safe, so far.

Her secret power is not her speed,
her teeth, or her claws.

It's knowing herself.

Knowing who she is
and where she should be.

From his skittish footsteps—
it seems the boy isn't so sure.

SNAPPER

"Let's ask if he wants to ride
with us sometime."

Kev and I look for snapping turtles.
I poke the pond with a stick.

"Ask who?" I poke harder,
pretending not to know.

No way would the Team
want me to ride bikes with Moses.

Riding with Kev is already stretching it.

The pond water is so dark,
I can't see a thing.

A tick crawls up my ankle,
and I smash it with my free hand.

DARK WATER

Dad says it's from the sandy soil in the pinelands.

Rain seeps through the loose grains,
leaching through rotted leaves

and pine needles, and into
the bogs, rivers, and ponds,

turning the water dark,
the color of tea.

The water is acidic.
It doesn't have many nutrients.

But you'd be surprised
what can survive there.

When an ancient snapper
breaks the surface,

I jump way back.
Its head is ugly and mean looking.

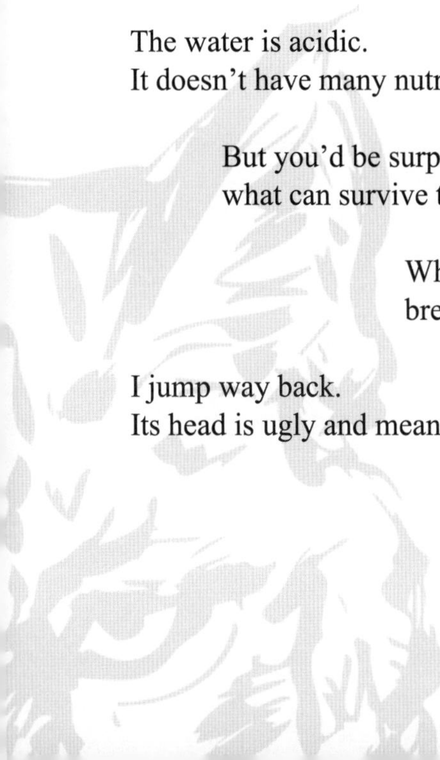

SATURDAY GAME

Everyone crowds around Mikey in the huddle.

After that, he throws the football straight
into a teammate's hands.

Mom gets hoarse screaming.
"Way to go, Mikey. Way to go!"

The cheerleaders keep shouting my
brother's name.

The next play, Mikey zigzags down the field,
carrying the ball.

It's his second touchdown in the first quarter.

We have the same last name.
But we're totally different.

No one ever calls Mikey "Hooser the Loser."

DURING HALFTIME

I spy on Mom, texting Dad on her cell phone.

Mom: You should be here!

Dad: Sorry.

Mom: You missed Mikey's touchdowns.

Dad: I'll be there next time.

Mom: Promise?

Dad: . . .

BLOB

In art class on Wednesday, Tomas comes up to me.

“You shouldn’t sit with them.”

He points at Kev and Mitzy. My face feels hot.

I hope they don’t hear him talking.

On Thursday, I sit next to Tomas.

My drawing is still a mess.

The bobcat looks like a blob with a curved tail.

I rip up the paper again. Kev keeps staring at me.

AUSTRALIA

It's just me and Dad on Friday night.

Mikey has a night game out of town.
Mom's working a double shift in the ER.

I cook healthy tacos for supper.

Ground turkey,
black beans,
corn,
salsa.

We eat in front of *Jeopardy.*

Best question of the night:
"The only continent with no active volcanoes."

"What is Australia?" we shout at the same time.

For one second, it's almost like
old Dad is back.

FIRE SLAYERS

While I'm babysitting Dad,
Mitzy and Kev see *Fire Slayers*, the new K-pop movie.

On Monday, they both wear
Fire Slayers T-shirts.

Three days in a row, Kev won't change his shirt.
Why doesn't Mitzy tell him it's not okay?

Didn't she see what happened to Moses?

STACKING STONES

I'm out on my bike,
riding past Mitzy's trailer.

Kev is in the clearing,
handing stones to Mitzy.

The pile is big, taller than Mitzy.
Then I see Moses.

He's stacking stones,
wearing his Mickey Mouse cap.

HOLD MY BREATH

At our next meeting behind the candy store,
Derek holds up his calculator
where he keeps track of everything.

“Out of one-hundred-twenty-five kids,
at least ten percent are weirdos,”
he says. “That’s twelve-point-five people.”

“How can there be a half person?” Alyssa asks.
No one answers.

When people start tossing out names,
I hold my breath, waiting for someone
to say Kevin Park.

But it’s not Kev.

KEEP QUIET

A kid on Lucas's intramural soccer team is messing up.

I mess up at soccer all the time. Who cares?

Lucas says Juan is making them lose games.

Derek agrees. "Our team could be number one."

"What do you think, Tomas?" Brianna says.

Tomas doesn't answer. He's on the team too.

I guess Juan had better watch out.

The rest of us just need to keep quiet.

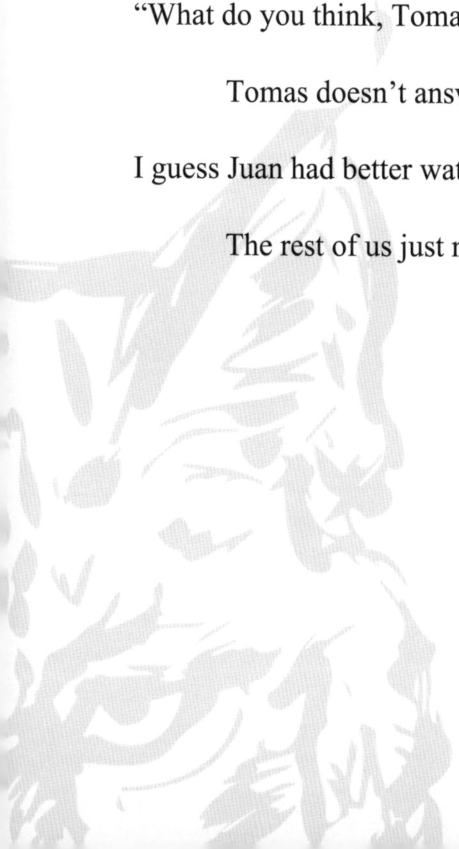

ON THE FIELD

When Juan misses a pass, Lucas bumps into him.

Hard enough to knock him over.
Hard enough for the gym teacher to take Juan out.
Not hard enough to injure him.

Tomas is watching Lucas,
and I know what he's thinking.

What if I miss a pass?
Will I be next?

LOYALTY

If Mikey knew, he'd be so mad.
He's always talking about loyalty.
"On the field, your teammates are all you've got."

I wouldn't know about that.
The Team is the only team I've ever been on.
I hear Juan quit soccer.

TEXT

Kev: For real?

Me: . . .

Kev: What did Juan ever do to you?

Me: It wasn't me.

Kev: Right.

Me: It wasn't.

Kev: Right.

THE TEAM

That's the truth.

It wasn't me, exactly.
It was Lucas.

        But it was the Team.

The Team isn't "them."
It's *us*.

If you're on the Team,
and the Team does something bad,

        then . . .

You do it too.

        Not you or them.
        But us and me,
        Charlie Hooser.

I am the Team.

SKELETON'S KNEES

Today, I pull
the Army blanket
off Dad's legs.

His bony knees
look like a skeleton's.

"I definitely
saw a bobcat," I say.
"I heard one too."

For some unknown reason,
Dad finally decides
to get up.

WALKING STICK

Dad squints in the sunlight.
He moves slowly, like it hurts.

I run back for his walking stick.
Dad grabs it with a shaky hand.

"Thanks, Charlie."

IN THE WOODS

Walking in the Pine Barrens with Dad
is like walking in the woods
with Henry David Thoreau.

You know Thoreau?
He lived alone on Walden Pond
and wrote about nature.

Dad can tell the difference between
a milk snake and a rattlesnake.
He knows which mushrooms are safe to eat.

I bet he'd love to live alone
in the woods like Thoreau.

It only takes a few minutes outside
for Dad to look better.

BOBCAT'S DEN

"What do you think a bobcat needs to live?" Dad asks.

"A lot of space," I say.

Dad nods. "What else?"

"Food . . . and a place to sleep."

He points to a stack of rotted logs.

"That's perfect for a bobcat's den."

Behind the logs is the Mr. Dangerous pile.

I walk faster, hoping Mitzy doesn't see me.

She might want to throw something at me.

"Everything okay at school, Charlie?"

"I guess."

KEV'S GRANDMA

is visiting from Korea.

She brought him a new pair of sunglasses,
and he wears them to school all week.

Kev's mom invites me over for supper.
I can tell Kev doesn't want me there.

"Introduce Charlie!" his mom urges him.

"This is my Halmoni," he mutters.

"You are a good friend to my grandson?"
she asks me at the table.

His mom puts more red spicy chicken
and vegetables on my plate before I can answer.

Kev coughs like he has a bad cold, which he doesn't.

HIDDEN

Mrs. Lopez hangs Mitzy's stone drawing
on the wall where everyone can see it.

The stones are many shades of gray
and all shapes and sizes.

It looks like a painting in the art museum in the city.

As for me, I have to start my bobcat drawing
over again for the fourth time.

When I stand up to get more paper,
I steal a look at Mitzy's new drawing.

I almost have a heart attack!

It's a blurry figure lost in the pine trees.
A human, but with wings and claws.

Half man. Half Jersey Devil.

REAL NAME

What’s his real name?
Mitzy won’t say.

But I hear her tell Kev
that Mr. Dangerous has been calling her mom.

I hope her stone pile
is getting taller than ever.

Mr. Dangerous is worse than the Jersey Devil
because Mr. Dangerous is real.

EMMA T.

Is it because Emma T.'s almost perfect?
She's friendly, gets straight A's,
and is really good at volleyball.

Or is it because of her braces . . .
(half the class wears braces,
so I don't know why it matters)

. . . that she's our
next target?

When I say that Emma brought
her lizard to school last year
and I got to hold it,

Brianna snaps,
"Lizards are weird too!"

WHAT WE DO

(And that means me. Charlie Hooser.
I do it this time. Maya, Alyssa, and me.)

We TP her locker.
Rolls and rolls of toilet paper.
Crunched into balls.

So much toilet paper,
it oozes from the opening
at the top of her locker.

It's just TP.
Easy to clean up.
It doesn't hurt anyone.

But when I see Emma T. waiting
for her mom to pick her up early,
she looks like she's crying.

PRINCIPAL SCHUMER

stands next to Mr. F in front of the room.

> "This is NOT happening again
> this year. I won't allow it.
> The next time I hear anything,
> anything at all, the entire sixth grade
> will be suspended."

Brianna whispers: "He can't do that.
My dad won't let him."

> I'm not so sure.

THAT GIRL

Why don't I stop Lucas
when he starts talking about Kev?

About his K-pop fandom.
About his blow-dried hair.
About how Kev is friends with *that girl.*

"She's weird." Lucas says.
"And that means *he's* weird."

Maybe it's because I'm starting to agree.

MEASLES

Mitzy IS weird.
No doubt about it.

What girl collects stones
to throw at someone called
Mr. Dangerous?

Brianna says weirdness
is like the measles.
"It's contagious
and has to be stopped!"

Maybe she's right.
Maybe the Team is right.

But that doesn't mean
I want Kev to get hurt.

THE FIRST TIME

I was Hooser the Loser was in second grade.
Back then I liked school.

I was always raising my hand.
"Good job, Charlie!" Mrs. Bevan would say,
when I answered right.

One day, Mrs. Bevan said,
"Good job, Charlie Hooser!"

Someone giggled.
"Charlie Hooser the Loser!"
And the whole class laughed.

Even Mrs. Bevan smiled,
before she told everyone to hush.

That was after Kev shouted,
"Shut up, you morons!"

Kev was the only kid who got a detention.

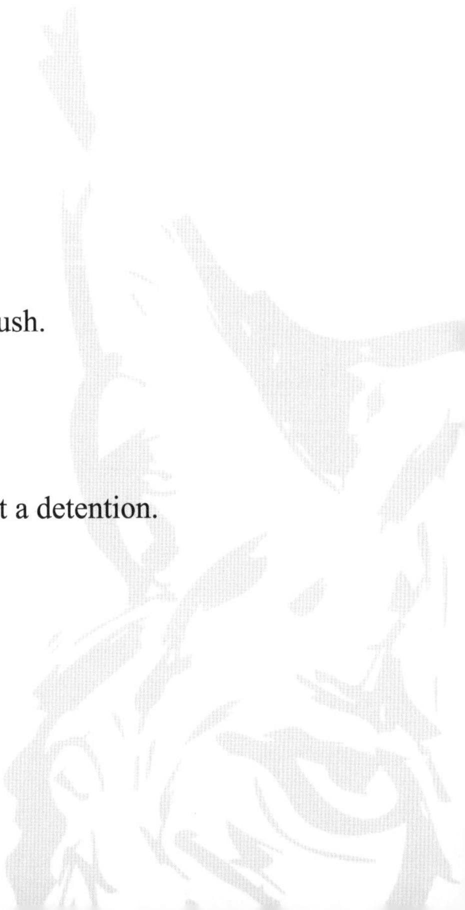

FRIENDS

"If I stay friends with Kev,
does that mean I can't be on the Team?"

I ask Tomas because he used
to be friends with Kev and me.

He had a mountain bike
and rode with us sometimes.

He stopped riding after he joined
the rec soccer league.

Kev and I were the only boys
in fifth grade who didn't play rec soccer.

Tomas shrugs. "Brianna says we're trying
to get rid of weirdos. Not be friends with them."

NO ONE'S

laughing at me anymore.

When Mr. F calls out my full name,
no one snickers.

I don't think they like me though.

A girl in math class moved her seat.
A boy refused to be my partner in science lab.

Even Mr. F is looking at me funny.

"Everything okay, Charlie?" he asks, after class.
"Your father feeling better?"

How does he even know about Dad?

DONE

And then Mr. F says,
"Some things you can't take back.
Once they're done,
they're done."

I feel my face get hot.
What does he know, anyway?

ELECTRIC GUITAR

Mitzy brings her electric guitar to school.
During indoor recess, she plugs it into the wall.

It’s a song from the K-pop movie.
I know, because Mikey listens to it all the time.

Kev dances and sings at the same time.
“La, la, la la, lalala.”

“Pipe down,” Mr. F says, pretending not to like it.

His fingers are tapping on his desk.

WHEELBARROW

Kev ignores me at school,
but he asks me to meet him and Mitzy
at the old iron furnace.

"Bring your dad's wheelbarrow," he says.

The old furnace is a mile up Route 9.

It's not easy to roll a wheelbarrow
on the shoulder of the road
with gravel spraying in my face.

I could be killed!

But if that's what it takes to keep
Kev talking to me,

I can do it.

IRON FURNACE

The Pine Barrens used to have iron furnaces
to melt the iron ore dug from bogs and swamps.
The iron was used for cannonballs, pots, and tools.

That was a long time ago.
All that's left are broken bricks, fallen stones,
and beer bottles from Friday night parties.

Also, rattlesnakes, broken glass, and rusty nails.
Dad tells us to stay away.
"Those places are dangerous."

"Come in!" I hear Mitzy shout.
Inside the ruins, she and Kev each have
a shovel and gloves.

STRONGER

Can sticks and stones
keep away Mr. Dangerous?

Can sticks and stones
help me keep my friends?

Back at the Mr. Dangerous pile,
Mitzy lifts a huge stone on top of a brick.

She's strong.
Stronger than she looks.

STICKS AND STONES

When Mikey and I were little,
Mom used to tell us the old rhyme.

"Sticks and stones can break my bones
but names can never hurt me."

Now I know the rhyme is wrong.

Sticks.
        Stones.
                Bad names.

All of them can hurt you.
All of them *do* hurt.

TRACKS

A clue, at last.

Fresh bobcat tracks, not far from Mitzy's trailer.

> Animal tracks are like fingerprints.
> They prove an animal exists.

Dad and I follow the tracks down a dead-end path.

"It's probably the last one," Dad says,
after his shirt tears in a bramble. "The last bobcat."

"How do you know?"

When we check again, the tracks are gone.

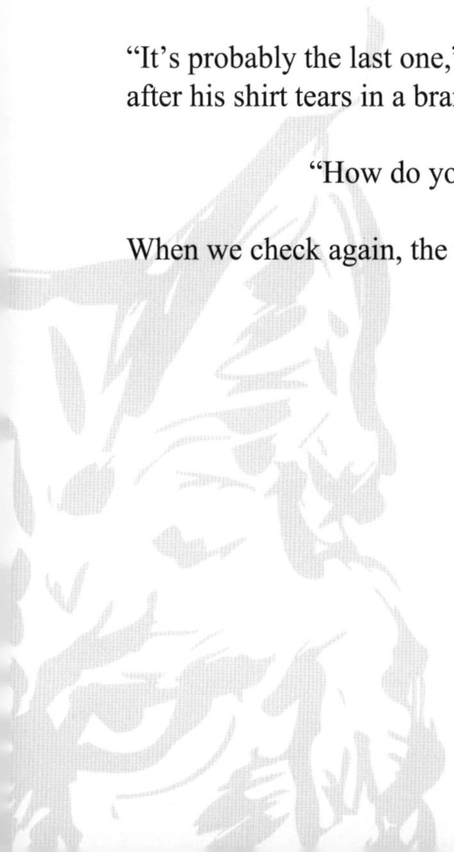

WE DON'T KNOW

if our bobcat is the last.

She could have cubs
or a brother
or a bunch of cousins.

If there's one bobcat, there could be more!

Right, Dad?

BOBCAT

The bulldozer crosses
into her territory,
crashing over logs,
leaving gashes in the sandy soil.

Her den is split in half
and then crunched into nothing.

She jumps over the stream
and skids into the mud
on the other side.

They're getting closer,
but they haven't gotten her yet.

A red-tailed hawk circles,
hungry for meat.

KEV OR MITZY?

“So which one is it?”

Brianna stares at me
with the iciest,
bluest,
deadest
eyes in the universe.

If I don’t choose, does that mean Brianna will?

But I can’t choose.
No way.
No how.

HOMECOMING

I don't know how Mom does it,
but Dad comes with us to Mikey's big game.
He even wears his green-and-gold team sweatshirt.
The game is tied in the third quarter.
Mikey already made two touchdowns.
Dad is cheering with the rest of us.
When I get a hotdog at the refreshment stand,
I see Kev. For the first time in a long time,
we hang out behind the bleachers.
Talking about nothing.
It's almost like old times.
At least for a few minutes.
Until Kev shouts,
"Charlie,
look
up."

TARGET

In the top row of the bleachers,

the Team is standing in a line,
looking down at us.

Kev and Charlie.

I start to raise my hand to say, “Hey!”

But I drop my hand when Brianna
lifts a large can over her head.

“What the heck?” Kev shouts.

It’s too late.

Pink paint flies through the air
and lands *SPLAT!* on Kev’s head.

PINK PAINT

Kev grips my sleeve.
Panting hard.
Shaking.

Gooey paint
drips down his face
and all over his *Fire Slayers* T-shirt.

"You tried to stop them, Charlie, didn't you?"

But I don't say anything.

"Didn't you?!"

And he takes off.

SCREAMS

Kev races into the parking lot.

I want catch him, to tell him it wasn't me.
To tell him I didn't know anything.

But I'm too slow.
I could never run fast enough.

As screams erupt in the stadium behind me,
my only true friend in the world

vanishes into a sea of cars.

MIKEY

is out for the season.

He fell hard in a scramble
and got a stress fracture in his left ankle.

Mom is quiet in the kitchen.
Dad’s TV is on full blast.

Mikey’s in bed,
his foot raised in a sling.

It’s like someone died,
even though everyone says

Mikey will be okay.
He’ll be back on the field next fall.

“Dad?” I say. “We have to go out!”

EVERY TIME

we take a walk,

every time we step over a wandering turtle,

every time Dad aims his binoculars
at a flock of ducks migrating over a bog,

or he stops to uncover
a tiny mushroom in a pile of leaves,

every time he's out in the woods,
Dad seems a little less lost.

It makes me feel good too.

"WHAT'S THAT?"

Through the trees,
a bulldozer lifts a pile of dirt.

Every year,
the pinelands shrink.

The protected Pine Barrens
can't be bulldozed,
but the wild lands
surrounding it
are turning into . . .

shopping strips,
new houses,
wider roads,

leaving less habitat

for mushrooms,
snapping turtles,
and bobcats.

"Those bozos!" Dad says and curses.
"They're ruining everything!"

BOZOS

Dad's back
on the couch.
"What's the use?" he says,
grabbing the TV remote.
"The bozos are taking
over the world."

HARD STONES

In art class today,
Mitzy waves me over.

For a minute, I feel hopeful.
But Mitzy's eyes are hard gray stones.

"You really are a loser, Charlie Hooser.
You weren't before, but you are now."

I never heard her call anyone
names before.

WHAT COLOR?

I haven't finished my bobcat drawing.
It's the eyes that stop me.

If you google a bobcat's eyes,
no one is 100 percent sure what color they are.

Some say yellow orange.
Others say gold.
One person says,
"The most beautiful eyes I've ever seen."

I'll never know if we can't find her.

A BIG MESS

Sometimes I think Dad is right.
The world is a big mess!

And then I think:

If Kev didn't act weird all the time,
he wouldn't get a can of paint dumped on him.

And if Mitzy didn't think I was a loser,
maybe I wouldn't be one.

Nothing makes sense.

BELIEVE IT

When Kev and Mitzy empty their trays in the cafeteria,

I can't believe what I see.

Kev is wearing a bright pink T-shirt.

So is Mitzy.

They dyed their Fire Slayers T-shirts pink!

"Weirdos!" Brianna says, loudly.

PINK

It only takes a week for half the sixth grade to turn pink.

Pink shirts.
Pink caps.
Pink sneakers.
Pink backpacks.

Boys and girls.
Cool kids and not-so-cool kids.

Brianna says, “What a bunch of losers.”

The word still stings
even though she’s not
talking about me.

CANOE

"Let's take the canoe out," Mom says.

We all look surprised.

Our family never does
anything together anymore.

At first, Dad says it's too much trouble.
Mikey's ankle hurts too much for him to go.

But when Mom asks again, Dad gets up.

And before he changes his mind,
I grab the paddles from the garage.

CATFISH

The dark river winds under low-hanging
branches and between sandy banks.
It's just wide enough for Dad's family-size canoe.

The turtles are missing on this cold morning.
We don't see any frogs or snakes,
but an osprey perches on a dead tree.

"Stop paddling," Dad says. "Shhh."
Minutes later, the osprey shifts,
lifts its wings, and dives straight down.

Splashing and churning, the river comes alive.
"Wow, wow, wow," Mom says.
A catfish dangles from the osprey's hooked beak.

K-POP POPS

After staying late to retake a math quiz,
I hear music in the art room.

I crack open the door.
Mitzy's playing her electric guitar
and Kev's doing flips.

Mrs. Lopez must have
let them push
the tables way to the side.

They're not alone.
The room is full
of kids waving their arms
and dancing in sync.

Even Mrs. Lopez
is stepping in line.

The banner on the wall says,
K-Pop Club Pops!

FORBID

Brianna forbids us to join the new club.
"If you do, you'll have to quit the Team."

She doesn't sound like a queen.
She sounds like a runner losing a race.

For a second, I think I'll join the K-pop club anyway.
It's a way out!

"Quitters are worse than losers,"
Glacier Eyes says, reading my mind.

LUNCH TABLE

Alyssa quit the Team today.

I didn't even know about it until lunch,
when only six people sat at our table.

Lunch tables hold eight people.
The empty chairs made me feel funny.

We're almost not a team anymore.

UP EARLY

On Saturday, Dad pulls me out of bed while it's still dark.

"I heard her last night," he tells me. "Let's hurry."

How did I miss the growls?

He hands me a flashlight and grabs his backpack.

"Maybe today's the day we'll find her," he says.

On the dark path, I run to keep up with him.

Dad doesn't need his walking stick anymore.

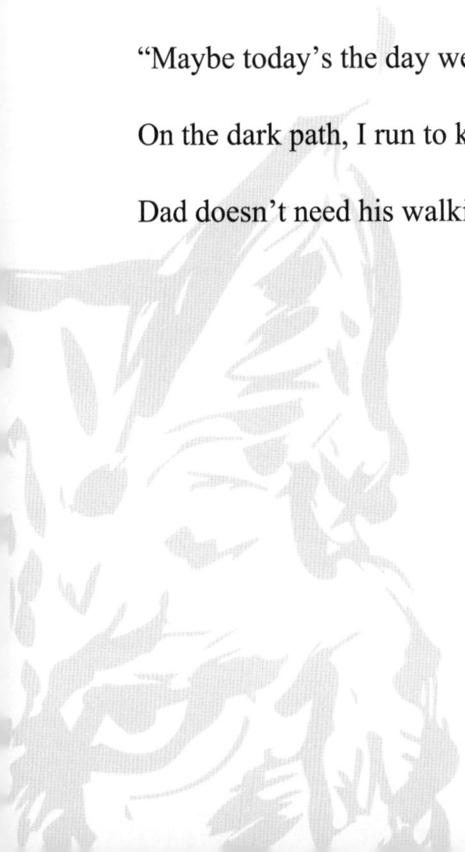

A BOBCAT

No one makes fun of a bobcat.
        No one calls her by any other name.

                        A bobcat is a bobcat is a bobcat.

But who is Charlie Hooser?

DAWN

As the light breaks, we look for the pile
of old logs, perfect for a bobcat's den.

The logs aren't there anymore.
All that's left are tire tracks and a big ditch.

"She's gone, son," Dad says.
"Maybe the bozos got her."

IN WILDNESS

"In Wildness is the preservation of the World."

That's Dad's favorite Thoreau quote.

I think it means:
If bobcats can survive, we can too.

But what if they can't?

NO-SHOW

On Thursday, Tomas is a no-show in the alley.

He doesn't tell us he's quitting.
He just quits.

Maya says she saw him at the K-pop club.

So Maya must have been there too!

Now it's just Brianna,
Lucas,
Maya,
Derek,
and me.

Brianna is eating mints like she can't stop.
Her ponytail's a mess.

She says we have to step up our game.

SALT WATER

Brianna has one idea after another.

Putting salt in Mr. F's water bottle
because he gave us a pop quiz on Monday.

Hiding Kyra's gym shoes because
her team won the relay race.

Spilling the janitor's soap bucket—
for no reason at all!

That was me and Lucas.
I kicked over the soap bucket.
Lucas threw the mop.

It was easy.

BEFORE SCHOOL

Everyone's dancing to Mitzy's phone,
except for Brianna.

She's got her head down.
Is she doing homework?

That would be strange.
I've never seen Brianna doing homework.

"Turn it up!" someone says.

Brianna's head falls so low
I think she might bump it on her desk.

The only reason the music turns off
is that Mr. F is rapping his knuckles
on the white board.

"Save it for after school," he says.

OBSESSED

Brianna can only talk about Mitzy.

About how she's going to scare her.
About how she's going to get her.

She's obsessed!

FIRE

Now Brianna's talking fire.
"A small fire. Not a big one.
Just to smoke them out.
Make Mitzy
go back to Brooklyn.
Where she belongs.
Don't you see?
She moved in and suddenly
everyone is getting weird."

Doesn't Brianna know?

There are no small fires
in the pinelands.
Not during a drought.

Dead trees stretch for miles
from the fire last spring.
Dad called that fire Armageddon.

A new fire could destroy everything.

NOT FIRE

"I won't do fire."

My chest heaves. I can't even breathe.

Brianna kicks the ground.
She's probably thinking:

If it isn't fire, what will it be?
What will Charlie have to do?

"Then you won't like this, either, Hooser," she says.

WHY?

I'm starting to wonder:
What's wrong with Brianna?

Why is she like this?

No big surprise.
Derek quits the Team too.

MOJO

Even after the canoe trip, Dad is blue again.

He still isn't going to work.
He still isn't the old Dad.

"He needs to get his mojo back," Mom says.
"The doctor says it takes time.

We can't stop trying, Charlie."

MUSHROOMS

One wall in the living room is covered with mush-
rooms.

In the bogs, meadows, and forests
of the Pine Barrens,
Dad snapped their photos.

He even labeled them:
lion's mane, turkey tail,
fairy helmet.

The only new mushrooms in our house this year
are on the frozen pizza Dad sneaks
when Mom's at work.

RED ONE

Near the snapping turtle pond,
a bright color catches my eye.

A red mushroom with white spots.

I've gone foraging for mushrooms
enough times with Dad.

I know where to look.

Back home, Dad grabs it from my hand.

He says it's poisonous and shouldn't be picked.
"You should know better!"

Instead of making Dad happy,
I just made everything worse.

"Bozo," he mutters.

I know he didn't mean
for me to hear that,

but I did.

CRYING GLACIER

Here's what happens today:

Brianna's in the parking lot.
Her father is shouting from a black BMW.

"Your grades are in the dumpster!
You really are stupid.
Why can't you be more like your sister?"

I never knew glaciers could cry.

ROYALS VS. LOSERS

Now I know . . .

The Team's not about clearing away weirdos.
It's about Royals vs. Losers.

Not just for me.
But for Brianna.
For all of us.

Brianna doesn't want to be a loser,
and I don't either.

No one does.

But is this how to stop it?

ANOTHER PINCH

Brianna grabs me in the hallway today.
Her fingers pinch my arm.

I hear one word.

"Mitzy."

MY TARGET

1. Pick the lock on Mitzy's trailer.
2. Smash her guitar.

"I hate her stupid *foreign* music," Brianna says.

"She's definitely weird," Maya agrees.

How can someone hate music?
How can someone hate Mitzy?

BIG DEAL

“What’s wrong with K-pop?” Lucas says.

Glacier Eyes grits her teeth.
“I hate that music. It’s stupid.”

Lucas laughs.
“I don’t see the big deal.”

He’s not scared
of Brianna anymore.

She laughs back.
“Well, you’re not doing it.”

She turns to me. “Charlie is.”

GOOD QUESTION

Mom keeps looking at me strangely,
just like Mr. F.

Tonight, she says, "I miss Kev."

When I don't say anything,
she asks, "Are you still friends?"

That's a good question, Mom.
I just shrug.

After supper, Mikey races me
down the driveway on his crutches.

Even with a bad ankle, he's faster.

"I told you to quit before it's too late.
But you didn't listen, bro."

I wonder if they both know how much trouble I'm in.

FAINTER

I hear the bobcat tonight,
but the growl is fainter.
I wonder if she's traveling.
Traveling away from here
like I wish I could.

MEANER

The Team wasn't always SO bad, Mikey tells me.

"They played silly pranks, but they didn't
really hurt anybody."

The pandemic changed everything.

The school shut down.
Some families lost their jobs.
Everyone was on social media.
It moved online.

"People got meaner," he says.
"That paint can could have hurt Kev!"

Mikey's right about one thing.
I'm definitely meaner.

FALL COLORS

The oak leaves are blazing.
In the swamps, the tall reeds
have turned gold.

I see a red-headed woodpecker
and a painted turtle
with its yellow stripes.

Wind hits my face.
My wheels
spin in the sand.

For a little while,
everything almost
seems normal.

RESPECT, NOT

A kid in the hall
steps aside for me.

Respect,
I think at first.

Then I hear
his friend whisper,

"Hooser the *Jerk*."

And the two kids both
rush away.

I'm not embarrassed.
I'm not angry.

I'll show them who's in charge.

Mitzy told Kev that she and her mom
are going away for the weekend.

Saturday night it is.

LADDER

Dad's TV is still on
when I push open my window
and jump out.

No, I don't fall off the roof.
Before dark, I pushed the ladder close.
Quickly, I'm on the ground.

Mikey doesn't even wake up.

Jumping on my bike,
the beam of my helmet lamp
leads me through the pines

to Mitzy's trailer.

WHAT I SEE

I see
a fallen pile of bricks and stones.

I see
sticks scattered like lost toothpicks.

I see
the trailer with the rainbow flag.

I see
the marigolds that Mitzy's mom planted.

I see
a strange car parked on dry pine needles.

I see
the New York plates.

I hear
the engine running.

I think:
Mr. Dangerous.

I SHOULD GO

Something is up. Could be dangerous.
I should go home,
not get involved.

I came here for a prank,
not a rescue mission.

But I remember how Mitzy took Moses's hand.

I remember how she's trying to keep her
mom safe.

I remember how I don't hate her at all.

And then I hear something fall.

NOW!

I knock on the door.

When Mitzy cracks open the door,
I look at her with a question
in my eyes.

"Call the police,"
she whispers. "Now!"

THE EXPLOSION

bursts our eardrums. Flames flare up.
The New York car's on fire!

Mitzy and her mom run out of the trailer,
followed by a man I've never seen before,

but I know exactly who he is.

I tap 911 into my phone while Mr. Dangerous yells,

"What did you do to my car?!!"

"He didn't do it. You did!" Mitzy cries, hugging her mom.

NOT DO

What you should NOT DO
during a drought in the pinelands:

Let your car engine run on a pile
of dry pine needles.

What a bobcat WILL DO when your car explodes:

Race across Route 9
just as three police cars,
an ambulance, and a fire truck
come speeding round the bend.

I SEE HER

She's like a torpedo shooting across the road.

I see her curved tail, fiery eyes, fast legs.

The cars and trucks are torpedoes too.

And I don't hear any of them brake.

A scream rips from my throat.

When the fire truck misses the bobcat by inches,

the terrible night goes black.

KEV

"Hey, Charlie, wake up!"

Kev is peering at me
as if I'm a dead frog in science class.

"A branch fell on your head," he says.

My head spins like an out-of-control merry-go-round.
I have a coughing fit from the smoke.

People are shouting.
Hoses are spraying everywhere.

Mitzy kneels next to Kev.
"You saved us," she says to me.
"But . . . why were you here?"

Kev says it's no time for questions.

"Eat this, buddy."

A cheese ball never tasted so good.

THE BOBCAT

"Charlie? Charlie?"
I hear Dad's voice calling.
Suddenly he's in front of me.
He's got on pajamas and hiking boots.
"I saw the bobcat!" I burst out.
"It was incredible," I tell him.
Then he hugs me hard.
"Oh, Charlie."

MR. DANGEROUS

I don't get a good look
at his face.

What I see are
the handcuffs
behind his back

as he's put
into a police car.

"He won't bother you again,"
the police chief tells Mitzy's mom.
"We'll make sure of it."

No one is happy tonight.

They're just relieved
nothing worse
happened.

So am I.

I'm glad we didn't have to use
our sticks and stones.

BANNED

Dear students, parents and guardians:

Due to disturbing reports of bullying and malicious pranks, the Team is permanently banned from Pinelands Middle School.

We encourage students to join clubs and activities that expand their skills and interests in positive ways.

We are a community. We stand with each other.

Sincerely,
Principal David W. Schumer
Pinelands Middle School
Pinelands, New Jersey

PASS THE LASAGNA

Mitzy's new house will be solar heated.
Her mom will have space for a vegetable garden.

Dad's team is already digging the foundation.

"Be sure you don't hurt the pinelands,"
Mitzy says. "I want it to last forever."

She and her mom are at our house for dinner.

"You've got my promise," Dad says.
"Now, please pass the lasagna."

LUCKY #7

K-Pop Dance Concert
7 PM, November 10, the Gym
Wear what you want to wear!

Moses wears
a Blackpink bucket hat.

Mikey lets me borrow
his lucky #7 football jersey.

Maya and Brianna wear
matching pleated skirts.

Mitzy turns up the amp.
Kev does a flip. The crowd
screams!

The gym floor bounces
like a million basketballs.

Someone hands me a lightstick,
and, before I know it,

I'm dancing in sync
with everybody else.

THE WEIRDEST THING

happens with my bobcat drawing.

I keep trying. I stop being afraid of failing.

On my sixth try, I sketch in a snapping turtle.

On my seventh, I add red-and-white spotted mushrooms.

A heron diving for fish.

Dad paddling his canoe.

Finally, I draw the eyes. The color of fire.

Mrs. Lopez enters my drawing in the art show.

It looks weird there, hanging on the wall.

This bobcat is part of me. But better. I'm going to be better.

"Charlie Hooser did that!" I hear someone say.

Yeah, that's right. I did.

Want to Keep Reading?

Here's a sneak peek at another book
from West 44 Books:

LIAM AND THE GIANT EELS
by Ann Malaspina

ISBN#: 9781978597549

THE GREEN CHAIR

The green chair
on the deck
stood empty.

No one touched it.
No one sat in it.

They pretended it wasn't there.

Just like the stuff
in Gramps's bedroom.

One evening in July,
a bird
landed
in the chair.

"Could it be an osprey?" Liam asked.

Gramps loved watching the ospreys
fly along Blackwater Creek.

"It's only a gull," Mom said.

One of a million scavengers
begging for scraps
at the Jersey Shore.

Bummer.

EARLY MORNING

at Sandy Cove Beach,

Pink bubblegum sky.

Joggers (including Mom)
on the boardwalk.

Matt the lifeguard, half-asleep.

Umbrellas opened
on the white sand.

And a flat, green, boring ocean.

WAITING

Liam floated
on his boogie board.

Waiting for
something—
anything—
to happen.

What a loser of a summer.

No waves.
No friends.
No blue crabs in his crab pot.
No Gramps.

A Jet Ski shot past Liam.

His board flipped
like a pancake.

"Way to go, Liam!"

Matt the lifeguard
put up his thumb.

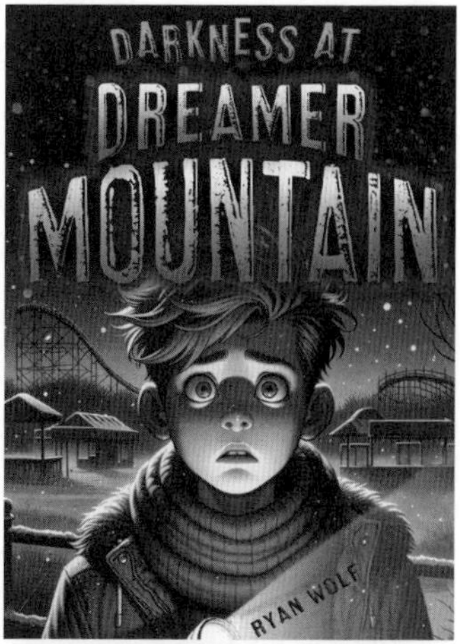

CHECK OUT MORE BOOKS AT:

www.west44books.com

ABOUT THE AUTHOR

Ann Malaspina has been obsessed with stopping bullies and saving wild places through her writing, ever since she got her first job after college as a newspaper reporter. In her spare time, she likes hiking in the Catskills and saving horseshoe crabs on the Jersey Shore. She's the author of *Ghost Runner, Liam and the Giant Eels*, and *Kiki in the Middle*, also by West 44 Books.